I Love You to the Moon

Antonio

By Suzanne Marshall

LiveWellMedia.com

ISBN: 9781094834092

This book is dedicated to

Antonio

who is loved very much!

~ *Antonio* ~

even if you were an owl

ready for sleep,

I'd still love you from

your wings to your beak.

~ Antonio ~

even if you were an elephant

napping at dusk,

I'd still love you from

your trunk to your tusks.

~ *Antonio* ~

even if you were a koala

sleeping like a log,

I'd still love you from

your head to your paws.

~ Antonio ~

even if you were a giraffe

much taller than me,

I'd still love you easily.

(I'd kiss you from a ladder or tree.)

~ *Antonio* ~

even if you were a bear

snoring loudly,

I'd still love you

very proudly.

~ *Antonio* ~

even if you were a bee

and really quite small,

I'd still love you

buzzing and all.

~ *Antonio* ~

even if you were a lion

with a furry mane,

I'd still love you

in sunshine and rain.

~ *Antonio* ~

even if you were a bat

with a tiny snout,

I'd still love you

inside and out.

~ *Antonio* ~

even if you were a polar bear

as white as snow,

I'd still love you

wherever you go.

~ Antonio ~

even if you were a panda

resting on a limb,

I'd still love you

through thick and thin.

~ *Antonio* ~

even if you were a kitty

sleeping sweetly,

I'd still love you

very deeply.

~ *Antonio* ~

even if you were a tiger

with a lot of stripes,

I'd still love you

morning, day and night.

~ *Antonio* ~

even if you were a puppy

dozing away,

I'd still love you

forever and a day.

~ *Antonio* ~

even if you were a bunny

who hops a lot,

I'd still love you

no matter what.

As you sleep, Antonio,

remember that:

I love you to the moon and back.

SPECIAL THANKS

to my mom and dad for their ongoing love and support, and to my awesome editorial team: Rachel and Hannah Roeder, Nathaniel Robinson and Don Marshall. Illustrations have been edited by the author. Original moon and stars were curated from freepik.com; clouds from medialoot.com. Original animals were curated from fotosearch.com: Bat, Bear, Bee, Bunny, Elephant, Lion, Owl & Panda: © Tigatelu. Kitty, Polar Bear, Puppy & Tiger: © Dazdraperma. Giraffe & Koala: © colematt.

ABOUT THE AUTHOR

Suzanne Marshall writes to inspire, engage and empower children. Her books are full of positive affirmations and inspirational quotes. An honors graduate of Smith College, Suzanne has been a prize-winning videographer and produced playwright. Learn more about Suzanne and her personalized books at: **LiveWellMedia.com**. *(Pictured below: Suzanne Marshall and her rescue dog Abby Underdog)*

Made in the USA
Monee, IL
24 April 2022

95312037R00021